1.00

GENERATIONS

For Cousin Bernice and the joining of

GENERATIONS

Selected Poems

Seymour →

Edited by Seymour Mayne
In Praise of Rachel Korn by Elie Wiesel

Translated from the Yiddish by
Rivka Augenfeld, Etta Blum, Morris Kirchstein,
Carolyn Kizer, Joseph Leftwich, Seymour Levitan,
Seymour Mayne, Leonard Opalov, Jess Perlman,
Howard Schwartz, Miriam Waddington,
Ruth Whitman and Shulamis Yelin

RACHEL KORN

Mosaic Press/Valley Editions

Canadian Cataloguing in Publication Data

Korn, Rachel H., 1898-
  Generations : selected poems of Rachel Korn

ISBN 0-88962-186-1 (bound). - ISBN 0-88962-185-3 (pbk.)

I. Title.

PS8521.076G46   C839'.091'3   C82-095065-3
PR9199.3.K67G46

Published by Mosaic Press/Valley Editions
P.O. Box 1032, Oakville, Ont., L6J 5E9, Canada.

Published with the assistance of the Canada Council and the Ontario
Arts Council.

The author and editor wish to thank the Jewish Community Foundation
of Greater Montreal for its support and encouragement.

Typeset by Speed River Graphics, Guelph.
Layout by Doug Frank.
Design and Frontispiece drawing by Sharon Katz
Printed and bound by Les Editions Marquis Ltee, Montmagny, Que.
Printed and bound in Canada.

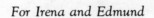

For Irena and Edmund

CONTENTS

In Praise Of Rachel Korn

Poet of the sufferings, wanderings, and memories of the Jewish people, Rachel Korn impresses and moves us with the evocative strength of her language. Each word calls out to us, each image burns itself into our minds.

Since I discovered her work twenty years ago, my warm admiration for her has continued to grow. Yiddish literature would not be what it is — and I would not be what I am — had Rachel Korn not opened the way for us.

Songs of exile and nostalgia, words of wisdom and courage, silent smiles and a measured vision — you read Rachel Korn and you discover a spellbinding world, dazzling and somber, peopled by a humanity that has died, yet lives forever.

No one else has her ability to paint the landscape of a buried village or her eye to portray the rapport between a mother and her daughter, between a vagabond and the sky, between a child and his longings. No one else has the grace to tell us what prompts man, wavering between need for peace and need for adventure, to imagine himself somewhere else.

Yes, I do love Rachel Korn. She is a great lady, the great lady of Jewish and world literature.

Elie Wiesel

Translated from the French

The Beginning of a Poem

It is fear, it is threat not to speak of,
It is standing on the threshold of pain,
It is the figure that looms in the doorway,
Shadowy, funereal, and gray.

It is genesis of firstness, the always,
It is the torrent that sweeps you away,
And makes you forsake all your dear ones
To welcome an awesome new love.

And all because some eagle-flying notion
Has seized you in its cruel sharp claws,
And holds you captive and torments you
To the last boundary of your breath

Until your blood is ready for the sacrifice;
Now nothing can save you from the angel's sword,
And nothing prevent your final going under
Except a lucky rhyme or somersaulting word.

Then all grows silent in your deepest self,
You hear the sound of every falling star,
And you become a delicate earthen vessel
Filled with the transparent flow of tears.

And you imagine: suddenly the world has ripened,
And earth is mother to the lonely wanderer's step,
God himself, you think, would have to worship
This ultimate, ecstatic, perfect moment —

And this is only the beginning of a poem.

Translated by Miriam Waddington

Summer Rain

Like girls yearning to be married, the overripe
acres of grain
wait for the singing wedding guests
who haven't come
in all these grieving days of summer rain.
They look up shyly as the summer sky,
its young head lost
in grandmother's soft grey cap,
weeps the melancholy fate of the fields.

Indoors since hay time,
sharp and shining
with the bridegroom's desire and joy,
the scythes wait for the sun's first smile,
the blessing
that will summon them to the wedding dance
on the full ripe brown fields.

Translated by Seymour Levitan

Berl's Cow

He sold the one-horned cow
and let the money blow through his fingers
like so much spiderweb.
Ever since, the stall has been empty
as the hole in a gum when a tooth is pulled,
The chain at the trough is rusty and cold,
and Berl's children haven't seen a spoonful of milk in the house
all winter.

When the woman next door milks her cow,
Berl's children stand around her like chicks
around a mother hen.
Ten pairs of eyes staring eagerly
at the warm white streams.

Berl goes to the market in town every Monday,
pokes the cows, examines their teeth, and bargains.
But it's always someone else who buys the cow.
Berl comes home
with a can of gasoline, kasha, and a sack of salt.

   Translated by Seymour Levitan

The Housemaid

The orchards of her home
still blossom in her glances
and in her dreams great flocks
of geese are feathered;
she used to drive baby geese
to the pond every spring
and guard them from the
crows and owls but now
for days she walks around
bewildered and her whole
body greedily drinks in
the fragrance from the new-cut
wood piled up by the stove
ready for burning.

Her faraway home was so
beautiful but it was a small
farm poor and rocky and
there were seven mouths
to feed so she the oldest
came to the city and here
her two hands are now the oars
which row her life through
dark and steamy kitchens.

When she gets a letter
from the neighbor's son
she runs to strangers
hanging on their glances,
first she reads their faces
for goodwill then begs them
quietly to read her letter,
to tell her all they
must tell all all that
he has written! Then she
sees their scornful smiles
at his loutish crudely formed
letters which for her contain
the alphabet of love,
and she blushes, hides her face
for shame.

All week long her heart
composes answers until
at last it's Sunday and
the words are put down
beside each other like
invalids on pink paper
decorated with doves
and wreaths of roses.
Her girl friend scribbles
the words in a hurry then
reads out whatever was
dictated ending with
kisses and respectfully
yours; she smiles fleetingly
and in the corners of her mouth
lurk the shy love words
she has nursed all week
and there they hover
captive and unspoken.

Sometimes in an hour of rest
she opens her old prayer book
with a gold cross embossed
on its black cover; with awkward
hands she caresses the strange
letters, words full of God
and love and mercy and her eyes
grow dreamy thinking about
the miraculous world of A B C.

The world she knows
is tied in a thousand knots,
even in the world of her prayer book
with its circles and lassos
is like some Judas: treacherous:
ready to sell her in a minute
for thirty hard days
of labour in every month.

Translated by Miriam Waddington

Crazy Levi

And no one knows what became of him, Crazy Levi,
who tied the roads
from Yaverev to Moshtsick
to Samber to Greyding in a bow,
carrying always in his bosom pocket
his letters to Rivtshe,
his uncle's youngest daughter.

All the houses in the villages know him,
the road accepted his long shadow
like a horse that knows its rider,
and the dogs lay quiet in their doghouses
when the familiar smell of Levi's flaring black coat tails
spoke to their hearts.

Women broken in the middle like sheaves
were in the field when Levi came by.
They toyed with him
and with a laugh that smelled of goodness, like dark bread,
they would say,
"Levi, you have no father or mother.
Why don't you take a wife
like the rest of your people?
She would wash your shirt for you
and cook you a spoonful of something warm for supper."

And Levi would look at their raw, swollen feet
and plow the brown field of his forehead
with the painful thought that was always present to him:
"Because my uncle wouldn't give me his daughter for a wife.
I carry my heart around
like a cat in a sack,
and I want to leave it somewhere
so that it won't be able to find its way back to me."

And he would take a filthy piece of paper
out of his bosom pocket
and read aloud from a letter in German,
"An Liebchen!"—
and a red berry would blossom
in the dark moss around his lips:
Levi's crazy, melancholy smile.

But after one long hard winter,
worse than any the old people could remember,
the small eyes of the windowpanes
looked for Levi without finding him
and the dogs put their heads to the ground
and sniffed at all the tracks on the road,
thinking he might have come by

And to this day, no one knows what became of him.
Maybe the hungry wolves in the woods tore him to pieces
or maybe his mother who hung herself in her youth
missed her son, and a small, white hand
reached out to him from the dark attic of the old house.

Translated by Seymour Levitan

I'm Soaked Through with You

I'm soaked through with you, like earth with spring rain,
and my fairest day hangs
on the pulse of your quietest word,
like a bee near the branch of a flowering linden.

I'm over you like the promise of surfeit
in the time
when the wheat comes up even with the rye in the field.

From the tips of my fingers my devotion pours on your tired head
and my years
like sown acres
become timely ripe and gravid
with the pain
of loving you, beloved man.

Translated by Ruth Whitman

I'd Love To Meet Your Mother Once

I'd love to meet your mother once
and kiss her hands.
No doubt she'd find you in my eyes
and all your words which I have cherished in my glance.

Perhaps she'd even come to meet me
with a smile so wise, so still
that always blooms on mothers' lips
when they see mirrored in the eyes of other women
their own passion for their son.

Or again, perhaps—
perhaps her look would warn me,
(mothers always know far more than other women)
of the wild grief
and the bitter joy
of loving her son.

I'd love to meet your mother once
and kiss her hands.

Translated by Shulamis Yelin

Longing

My dreams are so full of longing
that every morning
my body smells of you—
and on my bitten lip there slowly dries
the only sign of suffering,
a speck of blood.

And the hours like goblets pour hope,
one into the other,
like expensive wine:
that you're not far away,
that now, at any moment,
you may come, come, come.

Translated by Ruth Whitman

A Letter

You know, sweetheart—
today the day is as sunny and tart
as a yellow-gold fruit.
I'd like to take it
slowly and tenderly,
so as not to erase its translucent colour,
and wrap it in the soft flax of my dreams
and send it to you
like a letter.

But I know
you'd send the "letter" back immediately
with a note on the margin, all neat and fine,
that, I swear, you don't understand what I mean
(it's always like this with you, Rachel, always)
and you're angry
yes, you're even angry.
Because the envelope—is empty.

Translated by Ruth Whitman

Generations

for my daughter

Loving another, yet she married my father.
That other portrait faded with the years.
From her album paged in musty velvet
Shimmered forth his paling, yellowing smile.

To watch her embroider a towel or tablecloth:
She pricked the vivid silk with her nostalgia.
The stitches flowed like narrow streams of blood.
The seams were silvered with her silent tears.

And my grandmother—how little I know of her life!—
Only her hands' tremor, and the blue seam of her lips.
How can I imagine my grandfather's love of her?
I can will myself to believe in her suffering.

No letter remains, no, not a scrap of paper
Did she will us; only old pots in the attic
Crudely patched: tangible maimed witnesses
to a dead life: the young widow, the mother of five.

So she planted a luxuriant garden
That would embrace the newly barren house
And her new barrenness. So the trees grew,
Obedient to her will, in perfect rows.

Now my daughter is just sixteen
As I was on that quiet day in May
When I became pregnant of a single word
Scented with lilac, the remote song of a bird.

A few letters, and what is called "a slender volume":
These are the relicts of my life. I lacked perspective
On happiness, so I ran ever faster
To escape the happy boundaries of my fate.

Listen, my daughter, never go in pursuit!
It all lies *there*, in the woven strands of blood.
How the straight trees whisper in grandmother's garden!
Only listen! These dim echoes in my poem...

But what can sixteen years conceive of sorrow?
And pensiveness? the tremor of old lives?
For her, only the eternal beginnings.

Where she goes, old shadows kiss her footprints.
Somewhere, in white lilac, the nightingale
Gasps out his fragile song

Which ends always with the note of eternal beginning.

Translated by Carolyn Kizer

The First Line of a Poem

I fear that first line of a poem,
the sharp slash
that decapitates dreams
and opens veins
to a flood of blood.

Yet that line can bring me to the fields
moving in the wind to white, rose, and yellow
and the house under the tall pines
where no one waits for me any more.

It can take me to that hour
when memory is a dark knot
and on my hair I can still feel
the caress of hands that are no longer there.

Translated by Seymour Mayne
with Rivka Augenfeld

My Body

My body's like a tree trunk in the woods—
it stretches to the sky with all its branches,
its longing greens again
with each young love—

But my shadow
like a veil
stitched of thinnest mourning,
already takes my measure
for waiting earth,
for moist grass.

The summer day turns icy
in the hoop
of the narrow cask of shadows,
and the grass darkens
at my feet,
as though it were just touched
by a first breath
of autumn.

My shadow
like a veil
stitched of thinnest mourning
already takes
my measure
and sisters me
with waiting earth,
with moist grass—
and in my blood
I hear the world's weeping
and my unborn song.

May 1941
Translated by Ruth Whitman

On the Way

The flashing rails are prongs
stabbing the horizon
like a new-cut sheaf of wheat
ripened by the eastern sun

The train is a long black thread:
the sharp bright day
sews the distance with it
stitch by stitch.

For days and weeks
the bare brown sides
of freight cars
are home,
a shore
to homelessness itself,
to tears, to lice, to suffering,
and to me,
standing
in the centre of a desert,
facing the endless glare,
pawned by fate
and left as a pledge
to these horrible times —
a bundle of bones and a bucket of blood.

Ufa-Fergana, October 1941
Translated by Seymour Levitan

Arthur Ziegelboim

When was it sealed, when was it decreed,
Your great, your wonderful deathless deed?
Did it come to you like a child in your dream?
Or did a dark messenger bring you the tale,
In your London exile?

Did the messenger come to your door, and knock,
A woman heavily shrouded in black—
'I come from the Warsaw Ghetto, where the earth is on fire!'
Her clothes in rags, a tattered shroud,
And her lips red with blood.

Then you knocked at doors, and found hearts that were closed.
You tried to rouse them, but they wouldn't be roused.
What people were those who refused to listen,
When children were gassed and flung on the mound?
And no one raised a hand!

You carried round stacks of papers to show.
'You may be right,' they said, 'but how can we know?
We want to believe you. But these are not facts.
And we are bound by conventions and acts.'

You brought out a list of the dead.
'How can you prove they are dead?' they said.
So to convince them, you added your name to the list.
You always gave proofs, like a realist.

One May night, when the orchards ripened in the land,
And Spring walked around with stars, hand in hand.
One window in a London street showed a light.
That was you, sitting down alone, to write.

You wrote your last letters, and your last Testament,
For the dawn to read. before the night was spent.
Then a shot rang out, a single shot
To wipe out the shame of which you wrote.
You died to make the world listen to the cry
From the Warsaw Ghetto, across the sky.

Translated by Joseph Leftwich   29

The Watchman

Over ruined homes I stand guard
and over streets that are dead
where on crooked fences,
on walls crumbling one by one,
sorrow
hangs from the cobweb where it was spun.

The wind carries letters
to addresses now rubbed out...
A name flutters up,
long since unremembered, no doubt.

A shadow rises nearby
and climbs ever higher and higher,
to discover, if it can,
the very essence of a man.

In the tear-laden stillness,
despite a still unwept tear,
I am able to hear
the whisper of a confession
from underneath the shriveled earth.

*Translated by Morris Kirchstein
and Jess Perlman*

Sometimes I Want to Go Up

Sometimes I want to go up
on tiptoe
to a strange house
and feel the walls with my hands—
what kind of clay is baked in the bricks,
what kind of wood is in the door,
and what kind of god has pitched his tent here,
to guard it from misfortune and ruin?

What kind of swallow under the roof
has built its nest from straw and earth,
and what kind of angels disguised as men
came here as guests?

What holy men came out to meet them,
bringing them basins of water
to wash the dust from their feet,
the dust of earthly roads?

And what blessings did they leave
the children—from big to small,
that it could protect and guard them
from Belzec, Maidanek, Treblinka?

From just such a house,
fenced in with a painted railing,
in the middle of trees and blooming flowerbeds,
blue, gold, flame,
there came out—
the murderer of my people,
of my mother.

I'll let my sorrow grow
like Samson's hair long ago,
and I'll turn the millstone of days
around this bloody track.

Until one night
when I hear over me
the murderer's drunken laugh,
I'll tear the door from its hinges
and I'll rock the building—
till the night wakes up
from the shaking coming through every pane,
every brick, every nail, every board of the house,
from the very ground to the roof—

Although I know, I know, my God,
that the falling walls
will bury only me
and my sorrow.

Stockholm, 1947
Translated by Ruth Whitman

East

In this direction my father turned his face,
With his prayer shawl over his head.
Here are the fields and forests
He walked with firm tread.

My father's murmuring prayer,
That like autumn leaves fell,
Could take my wild blood,
My fierce passions quell.

Now I walk here alone,
The last of my race.
My grandfathers with their prayers
Made this a holy place.

And they and their grandfathers, too,
With their prayers and with their plough,
Dug themselves into this soil.
And the bond still holds now.

Under Poland's poplar trees
They dreamed of the Holy Land,
They planted here the mountains of Gilboa.
Here their Jordan ran.

We are coming back from far places,
From ghettoes, bunkers, crematorium fire,
The heirs of six million graves,
And we shall rise high, if not higher.

Translated by Joseph Leftwich

A New Dress

Today for the first time
after seven long years
I put on
a new dress.

But it's too short for my grief,
too narrow for my sorrow,
and each white-glass button
like a tear
flows down the folds
heavy as a stone.

Stockholm, 1947
Translated by Ruth Whitman

Lot's Wife

I wasn't brave enough to turn
when my home was burned
and my happiness was torn away.
I envy you
for turning in mid-flight
turning to salty stone
to guard the love you felt.

Fearing exile more than God's anger,
your longing was stronger than his hard punishing word.
Your home nested in your eyes,
cradle, orchard, flocks of sheep,
in that split-second when eternity conquered.

Now you watch over all your dreams,
and the bare mountains and the dead sea.
The blood trickles into your limbs at sunset;
reflecting the flame,
your body shimmers in the pink light, young again,
and you smile, remembering,
a smile of betrothal to your own name—
you are yourself again, no longer just your husband's wife.

I wasn't brave enough to turn,
and my heart turned to a clod of stone,
and the word turns to salt on my lips,
the taste of my unfinished tears.

Translated by Seymour Levitan

Put Your Word To My Lips

Put the word to my lips
like a signature at the end of a page.
Send me — where? I don't know —
for who waits there but the dark syllable?

I have been anointed with sadness
like the queen of endless night.
She does not know whether she is in a dream
or someone has imagined her.

Perhaps she has only been gambled away
to Fate's winning hand — wagered
as a stake and forfeited,
abandoned to the wind, to the unknown?

Put the word to my lips
and lead me like a child by the hand
to the border outlined by tears,
frontier at the country of night.

> *Translated by Seymour Mayne*
> *with Rivka Augenfeld*

Too Late

It is too late for the word
I chose for you,
yet perhaps it is too soon
for that stillness that opens
the distance between us.

There is no way now
to follow you —
the ash which was your glance,
the smell of your hair

have risen up again
with the planted wheat —
but the smoke
that rises and curls in the air
tries the sky,
becomes a chain,
and forms itself
into the letters of your name.

*Translated by Seymour Mayne
with Rivka Augenfeld*

I Fled From Desolation

I fled from desolation
And now I perish
Each day anew
Under skies drawn with smoke.

Lord, let me not fall so low
As to have to count consumptive hours
And be unable to look the sun in the eyes.

Buttress my dreams
With a pillow of stone—
Engraved with sayings,
Incantations against woe.

And send down an angel, stern visaged,
So that I need not struggle with myself alone,
While a starless night becomes desert about me
And into the distance there sinks a human moan.

Translated by Etta Blum

The Words Of My Alefbeyz

The words of my *alefbeyz*
smelled of wild poppies and periwinkle
ripe wheat and hay,
but they were branded with a number at Treblinka,
charred in the smoke of Belzec and Maidanek.

Mourning a last sigh,
cradling an unsaid prayer,
they are the messengers of the ghetto kingdom,
survivors of bloodbath and betrayal.

They inscribe me on synogogue walls
in unheard supplication.
Carved into me,
I am the gravestone of my people.

When was it, how many years ago?
Under the blossoming Cherry—
a wood bench, a table, a prayerbook,
points and lines like a new bridge
leading to the old shores of *tanakh*,

and all at once, as if struck by the scent of milk and honey,
three—
a wasp, a fly, a bee—
settled and drank at the edge of the book.

Stillness, only the humming wasp and bee,
when Shmuel, my teacher,
lifted the letters with his narrow ruler,
unchained each one from the long line.

The blue sky looked at the page
through the white petals of the tree,
gave a fatherly wink
to the doves on the roof,
and all rose circling one by one,
weaving a wreath of fluttering white wings
around my head

as if each dark word
on the half-yellow page
was a seed sown by God
for their greedy beaks.

Stillness now too— the quiet of evening
and only the page I write
stirring under my hand,
offering a home to my half-forgotten childhood
and my wandering.

Translated by Seymour Levitan

* *alefbeyz* — Hebrew alphabet; *alefbeyz* is the Yiddish pronunciation
**tanakh* — Holy Scriptures

Home

How many years have passed
since I stepped across the threshold
for the last time?

A bridal canopy of turbid smoke
has spanned itself
above my one-time home
with its wrought-iron rail,
and they who led me down the aisle to my beloved
are Belzec and Maidenek.

And I,
fugitive from under that black pall
am homeless still,
a wanderer,
nomad, with no guide,
a leper
scarred by adversity and pain.

My needs are few,
a corner,
a roof for my sorrow
which trembles
beneath the chilling glance
from alien eyes.

How many years have passed
since I crossed my own threshold
for the last time?

My days and nights grow dim
with premonition
that my home hangs
suspended on a spider-thread
of memory.

Translated by Shulamis Yelin

41

Nuns Who Saved Jewish Children

They are God's eternal brides,
These grass widows of the Holy Ghost,
Yet He seldom visits or brings news
Of their Mother Mary's grieving love.

They know Mary's downcast eyes
Only from the murals in their church,
Their own motherhood is parched and withered
And shrivels in their hands from drought.

But sometimes they escape on summer nights
Their fast of strictness and forget to pray,
Or hear the tapping of a child's hands
Against the locked doors of their cloistered hearts.

Then when morning comes and calls them all to penance
On convent floors laid out in brick and stone,
Their hair-shirts sting and stir the traces
Of all their dreams and hidden secret doubts.

And so in the hour when angels roam the world,
And mercy knocks at every gentle gate,
The nuns' hearts surely burst asunder
With the birth of a new kind of God,

And their billowing trailing robes —
Black waterfalls pouring through a wind —
Cool the shameful fires of Treblinka
And soothe a Jewish child's fevered head.

The homeless child's smile draws the sky
With all its light into their gloomy cells,
Their shy motherhood is fed and nourished
By the hunger of the child's starving hands.

When the nuns kneel down again to pray
Their words walk barefoot through the smoking ruins,
Their murmurous voices rise, grow luminious,
And light the darkness of a Jewish mother's grave.

Translated by Miriam Waddington

Memorial Candles

The days,
the nights,
lie down
layer upon layer,
upon layer,
when I measure time
with memorial candles.
Between one memorial and another
there is but one step,
through stillness,
through whisper,
through tumult,
as long as it took
to transform life into ashes.

Translated by Leonard Opalov

Keep Hidden From Me

Keep from me all that I might comprehend!
O God, I ripen toward you in my unknowing.

The barely burgeoning leaf on the roadside tree
Limns innocence: here endeth the first lesson.

Keep from me, God, all forms of certainty:
The steady tread that paces off the self

And forms it, seamless, ignorant of doubt
Or failure, hell-bent for fulfillment.

To know myself: Is not that the supreme disaster?
To know Thee, one must sink on trembling knees.

To hear Thee, only the terrified heart may truly listen;
To see Thee, only the gaze half-blind with dread.

Though the day darken, preserve my memory
From Your bright oblivion. Erase not my faulty traces.

If I aspire again to make four poor walls my house,
Let me pillow myself on the book of my peregrinations.

God, grant me strength to give over false happiness,
And the sense that suffering has earned us Your regard.

Elohim! Though sorrow fill me to the brim,
Let me carefully bear the cup of myself to Thee.

Translated by Carolyn Kizer

I Write Barely a Line

I write barely a line
and what I write I erase.
Here a letter is out of place,
here a stroke has gone awry
and here, found wanting, am I.
It may be
that I was lost, somewhere
in the folds of time.
There I was, sewed
with coarse stitches, as for a shroud.
Perhaps the knot can be undone
but only in the hour of grace
and by the hand of God alone.

Translated by Morris Kirchstein
and Jess Perlman

My Mother Often Wept

A birch tree may be growing on the mound
heaped by a murderer's hands
in thick woods near the town of Greyding,
and only a bird goes there to honour the dead

where my mother lies in an unknown grave,
a German bullet in her heart.
And I go, go, go there only in dreams,
my eyes shut, my mouth dumb.

I remember that my mother often wept,
and I, I imagined
Abraham's son, bound for the sacrifice, looking to her
from the pages of her prayerbook
while she lived Sarah's fate

and we tumbled, laughed, and played,
despite our father's early death —
Had he lived, our good father,
he would never, never
have taken us to Mount Moriah to be sacrificed.

And yet my mother wept so often —
Did she know
that heaven had prepared
to open wide its gates
and take her sons
in billowing clouds of smoke?

And I was left behind, her only daughter,
like a thorn in dry ground,
and I am the voice of my mother's tears,
I am the sound
of her weeping.

Translated by Seymour Levitan

46

Autumn Prelude

Eye, you are tired,
hand, you are, too,
heart, you are wearier still.
I may be wrong,
but are you fatigued by sorrow itself,
or even more by the tears
begging for a home in my song?

The sky is covered at twilight
with fever-red spots. But why?
Do leaves, falling from the tree of life,
smudge out all the blue
on all the stretches of the sky?

A cobweb quivers in the wind
and cradles in its netting
a drop of dew
heavy and clear,
as if an angel in his flight
had left behind a tear.

*Translated by Morris Kirchstein
and Jess Perlman*

With Poems Already Begun

With poems already begun
every line
pulls in another direction.
Each tries to trick me
into its own time and place.

Summer, autumn, winter, pass.
Only spring is hesitant
to appear here among these words
as if it were afraid
for its blossoms,

as if it were agonizing
whether to entrust
its treasures
and the promise of May
to my frost-silvered lines.

Translated by Seymour Mayne
with Rivka Augenfeld

And Even Words

And even words fade
under autumn's weight
and die in a final gasp
like the leaves under our feet.

This day of shame sweeps
together the fog of mountains and valleys
and covers exposed branches
and its own expiring face.

All the signs
I have read
in the clefts
of the earth
have fooled me —
I am estranged from the sky —
I am only close
to that great solitude
when the world around me
grows and matures
into the wisdom of silence.

> *Translated by Seymour Mayne*
> *with Rivka Augenfeld*

Blue Fog

Blue fog on the Galilean hills,
a scattering of stars,
and the full moon rules;
the whole sky is her's.

The moonlight falls on Kinneret,
and the waves curl pink,
as if a morning star, sunk and forgotten in the water,
were waking from his dreams.

In a courtyard, the sad unearthly
sobbing of a donkey —
dreaming
his heavy burdens of the day to come.

And bats circle, circle, circle
over water, hill, and tree,
as if the night were shooting arrows,
dark arrows into the hidden heart of dreams.

Translated by Seymour Levitan

Tiberias

She bears a foreign name,
sign of imperial Rome
and the hard soles of sandals
that stifled her — proud Tiberias!

pawned to patrician matrons,
to bathe their feet and serve —
Weeds grow in the crumbling walls
of the Roman ruins bare to the sky.

The mouths of caves in the hills
begin to tell an old tale,
and in the blue silence beyond time
young voices and a thread of song,
    O Kinneret Mine.

The water shimmers pink where the moon shines,
and Kinneret drinks the words like wine,
drunk with silent grief
for her pale, silent maidservant.

    Tiberias, December 1965
    Translated by Seymour Levitan

The Thirty-one Camels

Thirty-one camels
trudge through the white burning sands
of the Sahara,
laden with the load
of my longing,
the treasure of my sacred hope.

Against them
Sahara stretches her feverish brown body
indolent and weary.
Eagles fly over her with flaming wings
and lions soothe her with lullabies
on starry nights.

Thirty-one camels
trudge among white caravans
of bleached skeletons
with annihilation
in their eyes.

Thirty-one camels
make their way
without a leader,
without a guide.

Translated by Howard Schwartz

Last Night I Felt A Poem On My Lips

Last night I felt a poem on my lips,
a luscious fruit, sweet and tart,
but it dissolved into my blood at dawn,
all but its smell and color gone.

I hear the quiet pulsebeat in the stammering of things
that might have come into the open,
abandoned, their heart shut tight,
and no pleading now will lure them out.

Every part of me has died an early death,
my head is bowed in mourning to the ground.
God called me to renew Creation
and I failed to hear His word.

The day paled at the start.
God's face is covered with a cloud.
Left with a barren sheet of paper in my hand,
I stand shamed at my door
like a stranger.

Translated by Seymour Levitan

Everything Lonely Has The Color Of My Grief

Everything lonely has the color of my grief,
everything shamed and tired
stands in a crown of extinguished stars
at the first word of my poem.

Lost beggars, outcast princes,
forgotten smiles, unwept tears —
who will bow and invite you in,
all of you, when I'm gone?

Translated by Seymour Levitan

By the Lake

In the morning by the lake
the undulating fog like script
writes over the sharp exclamation point
of a black crow.

Too bad. The story still remains to be told —
the story the stillness invented
and entrusted to dawn-gray fogs
at the edge of an August night.

Only the September leaves,
brittle and desiccated,
rustle
when the heavy dew
drips from them —
drop after drop after drop.

Translated by Seymour Mayne
with Rivka Augenfeld

From Here to There

From here
to there —
is it far?
Just a step.

Everything is prepared,
all is ready:
even the angel
with wings folded
like tired arms,
waits at the crossroads of time
to kiss my forehead —

that I should
forget all,
that I should become
like him,
without smile,
sadness,
or tears.

Translated by Seymour Mayne
with Rivka Augenfeld

Notes on the Author

Rachel Korn was born in 1898 in the village of Podliski, East Galicia. Her first poems and stories appeared in Polish. Since 1919 she has written all her work in Yiddish. During World War II she fled to the Soviet Union where she remained for a number of years until she immigrated to Canada.

In 1966 a selection of her writings appeared in Hebrew translation. Canadian, American and British translators have rendered many of her poems and stories into English. Her work has also been translated into French, German, Polish and Romanian, and she is represented in numerous anthologies including *The Treasury of Yiddish Poetry, Canadian Yiddish Writings, The Penguin Book of Women Poets, The Poets of Canada, Voices Within the Ark: The Modern Jewish Poets,* and *The Spice Box: An Anthology of Jewish Canadian Writing.* Rachel Korn has received such prestigious literary awards as the Lamed Prize for both poetry and prose, the H. Leivick Prize, the I. Manger Prize, and the Award for Yiddish Poetry from the Jewish Book Council of the United States.

Much of what she has written finds its source in her formative years in Poland, her wanderings during and after World War II, and the loss of the vibrant Eastern European Jewish world in the Holocaust. Her poems of Canada, also haunted by loss, sketch the darker seasons and complement her more hopeful lyrics depicting the landscape of Israel. Since 1948 Rachel Korn has lived in Montreal.

Unfortunately, Rachel Korn died on September 9, 1982, as this book was going to press.

Books by Rachel Korn

In Yiddish

Village
   (Poems, Vilna, 1928)

Earth
   (Short Stories, Warsaw, 1936)

Red Poppies
   (Poems, Warsaw, 1937)

Home and Homelessness
   (Poems, Buenos Aires, 1948)

Kismet: Poems 1928-1948
   (Poems, Montreal, 1949)

Nine Stories
   (Short Stories, Montreal, 1957)

On the Other Side of the Poem
   (Poems, Tel Aviv, 1962)

The Grace of the Word
   (Poems, Tel Aviv, 1968)

On the Edge of an Instant
   (Poems, Tel Aviv, 1972)

Altered Reality
   (Poems, Tel Aviv, 1977)

In Translation

Poems and Earth
   (Poems and Prose, Tel Aviv, 1966)
   Translated into Hebrew by Shimshon Meltzer

ACKNOWLEDGEMENTS

"I Fled from Desolation" translated by Etta Blum and reprinted from *A Treasury of Yiddish Poetry*, eds. Irving Howe and Eliezer Greenberg, Holt, Rinehart and Winston, New York, 1969. Used by permission.

"The Watchman," "I Write Barely a Line," and "Autumn Prelude" translated by Morris Kirchstein and Jess Perlman. Used by permission of Jess Perlman.

"Keep Hidden from Me" and "Generations" translated by Carolyn Kizer and reprinted from *A Treasury of Yiddish Poetry*, eds. Irving Howe and Eliezer Greenberg, Holt, Rinehart and Winston, New York, 1969. Used by permission.

"East" and "Arthur Ziegelboim" translated by Joseph Leftwich and reprinted from *An Anthology of Modern Yiddish Literature*, ed. Joseph Leftwich, Mouton, The Hague, 1974. Used by permission of Joseph Leftwich.

"Summer Rain," Berl's Cow," "Crazy Levi," "Lot's Wife," "My Mother Often Wept," "Blue Fog," "Tiberias," "Last Night I Felt a Poem on My Lips" and "Everything Lonely Has the Color of My Grief" translated by Seymour Levitan and reprinted from *Jewish Dialog*. Used by permission of Seymour Levitan.

"On the Way" and "The Words of My *Alefbeyz*" translated by Seymour Levitan and used by permission of the translator.

"The First Line of a Poem," "Put Your Word to My Lips," "Too Late," "With Poems Already Begun," "And Even Words," "By the Lake" and "From Here to There" translated by Seymour Mayne with Rivka Augenfeld and reprinted from *Jewish Dialog*. Used by permission.

"Memorial Candles" translated by Leonard Opalov and used by permission of the translator.

"The Thirty-one Camels" reprinted from *Voices Within the Ark: The Modern Jewish Poets* by permission of Howard Schwartz. Translation copyright (c) 1979 Howard Schwartz.

"The Housemaid" translated by Miriam Waddington and reprinted from *A Treasury of Yiddish Poetry*, eds. Irving Howe and Eliezer Greenberg, Holt, Rinehart and Winston, New York, 1969. First broadcast over C.B.C. and used by permission of Miriam Waddington. Translation copyright (c) 1982 by Miriam Waddington.

"The Beginning of a Poem" first broadcast over C.B.C. and "Nuns Who Saved Jewish Children" first published in *Viewpoints*, used by permission of Miriam Waddington. Translations copyright (c) 1982 by Miriam Waddington.